Enid Blyton's
NODDY
and the Broken Bicycle

BBC CHILDREN'S BOOKS

Noddy's best friend, Big-Ears, was coming to dinner, and Noddy was planning a special meal.

"I've got radishes and parsnips, so I think I'll make radish and parsnip stew!" he said.

Just then came a knock on the door, and in walked Mrs Tubby Bear.

"Noddy," she said, "have you heard the news? Big-Ears has cycled straight into Jumbo, the toy elephant! Poor Big-Ears has fallen off and hurt his head, and Jumbo has sat down on the bicycle. It's smashed to bits!"

"I must go to him at once!" said Noddy.

Big-Ears' bicycle was completely ruined, and Jumbo was feeling rather sorry for himself.

"He was going at a hundred miles an hour and he didn't even ring his bell," he muttered. "Whatever next?"

Big-Ears was sitting down, looking very unhappy.
"My poor bicycle!" he said. "My poor bicycle!"
"Don't worry, Big-Ears," said Sally Skittle. "Look!
Here comes Noddy!"

"Are you all right, Big-Ears?" asked Noddy. "I've come to take you home with me. Come along now."

"Ooh! Aah! Ooh!" cried Big-Ears, painfully. He was very bruised and his head hurt.

"Don't worry," said Noddy. "You will soon be in bed."

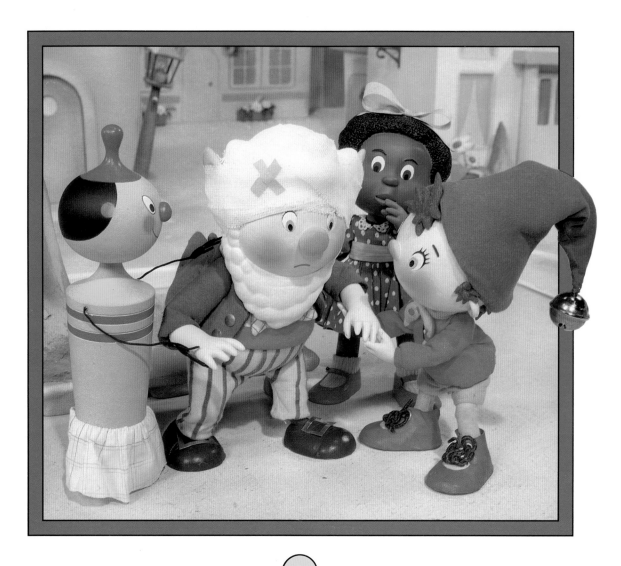

"I'll never be able to pick all these bits off,"
grumbled Jumbo, as he walked away.
"They are making a terrible noise."

"Oh, Jumbo!" laughed Noddy.
"The bicycle bell is stuck to
your tail! Let me take it off
for you."

At last, Big-Ears was tucked up in bed. "All I have left is my bicycle bell," he said unhappily.

"Remember what the doctor told you," said Noddy. "YOU MUST NOT WORRY!"

"Please don't shout," said Big-Ears.

"I'm sorry, Big-Ears," whispered Noddy. "I shall tiptoe away and let you rest quietly. But remember, YOU MUST NOT WORRY!" he boomed.

Big-Ears just groaned and held his head.

"Oh, I am sorry!" whispered Noddy.

Noddy was wondering how he could help Big-Ears to buy a new bicycle. "N-no, that idea's no good . . . Perhaps – oh, no, that's no good either," he said. As he was trying to decide what to do, Mrs Tubby Bear came hurrying up.

"I am glad that I've found you," she said. "I have a message for you. Farmer Straw wants you to drive to his farm in your car, pick up his sacks of potatoes, and deliver them to Goblin Corner."

"I can do that right away while Big-Ears is resting,"
said Noddy, cheerfully. "He needs some peace and quiet!
What should I do with the sacks when I get there?"
he asked.

"Just leave them for the farmer's brother to collect," said Mrs Tubby Bear. "Farmer Straw is going to pay you seven sixpences!"

"You will be rich, Noddy!" said Mr Tubby Bear as he walked up.

"I'm going to buy Big-Ears a new bicycle," said Noddy. "He will be thrilled!"

Big-Ears was delighted when
Noddy returned and told him
what he had done.

"Thank you, Noddy," he smiled.
"You are very kind."

Just then, Mr Plod marched in.

"Noddy," said Mr Plod, sternly. "Did you steal six sacks of potatoes from Farmer Straw today?"

"Of course I didn't steal them," cried Noddy.

"Pink Cat saw them in your car. Where are they? Are they here?" demanded Mr Plod.

"Stop being silly, Mr Plod," said Mrs Tubby Bear. "Noddy didn't *steal* them. A goblin asked me to tell Noddy that Farmer Straw wanted him to move the sacks to Goblin Corner."

"A goblin!" cried Noddy. "They're always playing tricks on me!"

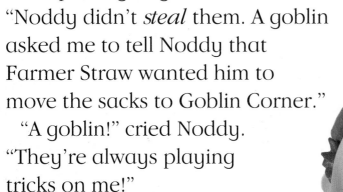

"Well, *you* took the potatoes, so *you* must pay for them," said Mr Plod.

"I'll pay," said Noddy. "I shall open my money-box. But don't worry, Big-Ears. I shall go to Goblin Corner tonight and catch the thief when he comes to collect the sacks!"

That night, when it was dark, Noddy went to Goblin Corner to see who would come and steal the sacks of potatoes. He was hiding up in the old oak tree, watching carefully.

"Brrr! It's cold!" said Noddy, shivering. "I hope I won't be here for very long. I want to go home and get into my nice warm bed! Hurry up, thief!"

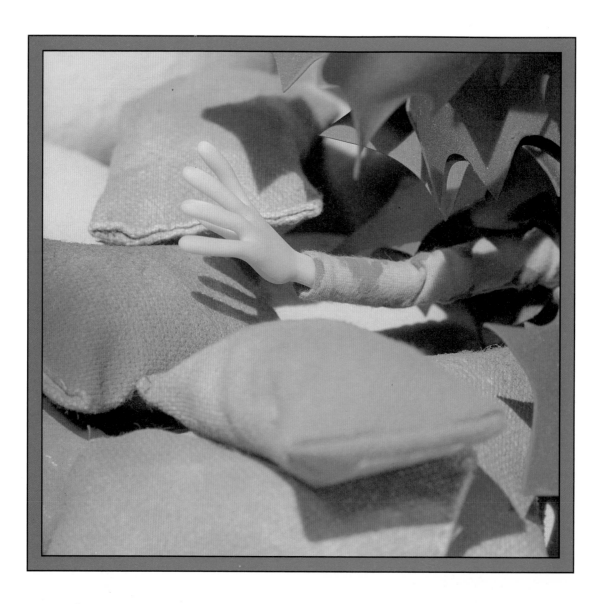

At that very moment, Noddy thought he heard a rustling noise. Down beneath the bushes there was a hand reaching stealthily for the sacks. The thief was there!

"What's that noise?" thought Noddy. "Oh! The thief has come for the potatoes! Well, I'm going to catch him and find out who it is, and take him straight to Mr Plod!"

Noddy jumped right out of the tree, and landed on top of the naughty goblin.

"I've got you now!" he cried. "Come with me! You're going to prison!" Noddy pulled the goblin over to his car.

The little car switched on its headlamps, and Noddy was able to see who had played the nasty trick on him.

"Good gracious!" he said. "Sly the goblin! *You're* the potato thief!"

"Mercy! It was only a joke!" cried Sly.
"Please don't take me to Mr Plod!
I don't want to go to prison.
I – I'll make a spell for you!
I'm good at spells. Is there
anything you want?"
  Noddy had a very
clever idea.

"Can you make Big-Ears a new bicycle?" asked Noddy.

"If I had one of the pieces, then I could work a spell on that," said Sly.

"There *is* something left," said Noddy. "We've still got the bell! Come along, Sly!"

It was very late indeed when they arrived at House-for-One, but Big-Ears was still waiting for Noddy to return.

"What a surprise he will have!" thought Noddy to himself.

Big-Ears *was* surprised when Noddy told him what Sly was going to do. They put the bicycle bell in the middle of the floor, and watched as Sly started to make his spell.

"Bicycle bell, I'll weave you a spell.
Bicycle-magic is in it.
Grow, grow, two wheels in a row.
It won't take you more than a minute!

Make, make, pedals and brakes,
Tyres and handlebars too.
Bicycle bell, I'll weave you a spell.
Hollabee, rinnabee, HOO!"

There was Big-Ears' bicycle!

"My bicycle's all right again! My bicycle's all right!" cried Big-Ears. He was so delighted that he didn't even care that Sly was creeping away.

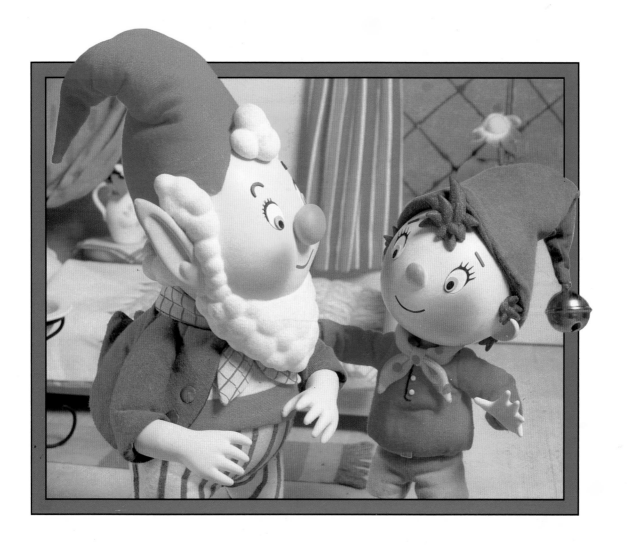

"I don't even have to put the bell back on," he said happily. "Everything is all right now!"

"You see?" said Noddy. "I *told* you not to worry!"

Big-Ears laughed and laughed and laughed!

Other Noddy *TV Tie-in titles*
available from BBC Children's Books

Published by BBC Books
a division of BBC Worldwide Publishing
Woodlands, 80 Wood Lane, London W12 0TT
First published 1993
Reprinted 1994 (three times)
Reprinted 1995
Text and stills copyright © BBC Worldwide Publishing 1993
ISBN 0 563 36865 9

Based on the Television series, produced by Cosgrove Hall Productions, inspired by the Noddy Books
which are copyright © Darrell Waters Limited 1949–1968

Enid Blyton's signature and Noddy are Trademarks of Darrell Waters Limited

Typeset in 17/21 pt Garamond by BBC Books

Printed and bound in Great Britain by Cambus Limited, East Kilbride
Colour separations by DOT Gradations, Chelmsford
Cover printed by Cambus Limited, East Kilbride